Cats
by the
Side of the
Road

AUTHOR **FRANKIE DOVEL MORRIS**

ILLUSTRATOR **ERIN DOVEL**

Archway Publishing books may be ordered through booksellers or by contacting:

Archway Publishing
1663 Liberty Drive
Bloomington, IN 47403
www.archwaypublishing.com
1 (888) 242-5904

Graphics by Erin Dovel

ISBN: 978-1-4808-1888-0 (sc)
ISBN: 978-1-4808-1889-7 (e)

Print information available on the last page.

Archway Publishing rev. date: 6/12/2015

To John(ny) – a gentle and caring husband, father, grandfather, uncle and brother - a kind protector of animals.

And to Barbara – our shining star.

Marcia stopped at the gas station to put gas in her car. As she walked around the gas pump she heard, "Meow, meow, meow," in a high, scared voice. She saw a small black and white cat.

"Move away from the pump, little kitty, move away!" Marcia said in a worried voice. "You'll be hit by a car if you stay here."

When Marcia went into the gas station to pay for the gas, she bought a large can of cat food. "Maybe I can get the cat to move away from the pump to a safer place," she thought.

When Marcia went out to the pump the cat was gone. She looked around and saw the small cat next to a grassy patch in the parking lot of the gas station.

Marcia opened the can of cat food and called, "Here kitty, kitty, kitty," but the cat ran away as Marcia got closer. "It's O.K. kitty, kitty – I'll leave the can here for you," said Marcia in a soft voice. The cat stopped at the sound of her voice, turned and watched Marcia as she placed the open can of food near the grass.

As Marcia slowly walked away, the little cat cautiously approached the opened can of cat food. When the cat reached the can, she could smell its contents, so she quickly started to eat. The entire time she ate, she never took her eyes off of Marcia. The little black and white cat was afraid of Marcia.

Finally, Marcia got in her car and left the little cat by the side of the road. When Marcia got home she couldn't stop thinking about the poor little black and white cat. She decided that she would start feeding the cat every evening.

Marcia was worried because the cat was in a dangerous location. The gas station was on a busy road and the little cat only had a small patch of grass and the woods beside the gas station as a place to live.

Marcia went back to the gas station the next day with more cat food but she didn't see the black and white cat. She called, "Here kitty, kitty, kitty, kitty," and off in the distance she heard, "meow, meow, meow." "Is it possible that I hear the little cat answering me?"

She called again, "Here kitty, kitty, kitty, kitty," and again she heard a little louder, "Meow, meow, meow." Then the little cat ran out from the edge of the woods.

"Hi little kitty," said Marcia in a soft voice. "I can't believe that you came when I called! Good to see you little kitty. Do you want some food?"

The little kitty was careful to stay a safe distance away from Marcia. The cat was nervous but excited as she continued to meow without stopping. "Meow, meow, meow," continued the little cat as Marcia quickly opened the can of food and backed away so that the little kitty would eat.

The next day when Marcia went to feed the little cat, she took two cans of cat food because Little Kitty always seemed so hungry. The little cat ate both cans of food and as she ate, she always kept her eyes on Marcia. Marcia sat on the curb next to the grass and talked softly with Little Kitty as she ate. Little Kitty was letting Marcia get closer.

When Little Kitty finished eating her two cans of cat food, she didn't run back into the woods. Little Kitty sat on the grass and looked at Marcia, sometimes saying, "meow, meow, meow," which Marcia thought was "thank you," in cat language.

Everyday Marcia went to feed Little Kitty in the evening and every time Little Kitty was there waiting on the grass at the edge of the woods.

Then one day when Marcia arrived at the gas station, Little Kitty ran out of the woods crying "Meow, meow, meow," but she didn't eat. She cried, "Meow, meow, meow," again and two kittens came running out of the woods. One kitten was very small and all black. The other one looked exactly like his mother.

What a surprise – Little Kitty had two kittens!

Marcia was very surprised to see the kittens. All three cats shared the same bowl and Marcia was glad that she had brought extra food!

Every day Marcia took food to Little Kitty and her kittens. She would put down the three bowls of food and the cats would run out from the woods and eat. After eating the kittens would chase a stick that Marcia would pull along the ground while the mother, Little Kitty (now mama cat), watched from a distance.

Marcia knew that she had to make a plan to catch the cats and remove them from this dangerous area. She contacted an organization called "Voices of Animals" and went to a training session so she could learn to trap the cats.

Marcia got three traps. She decided to try and trap the cats when she went to feed them. When she arrived, all three cats were waiting for her as usual. Instead of putting food down, Marcia placed the three traps on the ground with the food inside the traps.

Almost immediately the two kittens went into their traps. Marcia waited and waited and waited, hoping that the mama cat would go into her trap to get the food but Mama Cat just looked at the food.

Marcia put the traps with the two kittens in the back of her car. She kept talking softly to Mama Cat trying to get her to go into her trap. Mama Cat walked around the trap and even sat on the top of the trap but she didn't go in.

It got dark and still Marcia had not trapped Mama Cat. Marcia waited and waited. Mama Cat didn't go back into the woods but she didn't go into the trap either. She just kept looking at Marcia and saying, "meow, meow, meow." She was looking for her kittens.

Marcia sat quietly looking at Mama Cat for a long, long time and then Mama Cat walked closer to the trap. "Please go into the trap," thought Marcia. "Please, please, please."

And then it happened – the mama cat went in the trap and the trap door snapped shut.

Marcia felt so happy when she put Mama Cat in her car with the kittens. Then Marcia promised, "You will never come back to this dangerous area and I will find good homes for all of you," and Marcia was able to keep her promise.

epilogue

Today Mama Cat lives with the author. Quiki, the little boy kitten and his sister Luna, live with a family in the Charlottesville area. All three cats are doing very well.

Frankie Dovel Morris teaches English as a second language and she enjoys using books to support learning. She hopes parents will read *Cats by the Side of the Road* with their children to improve awareness of and advocacy for abandoned animals. She lives in Charlottesville, Virginia.

Erin Dovel grew up in Freehold, New Jersey, and earned a master's degree in civil engineering from Villanova University. She works in engineering but still has time to nourish her love of art through her beautiful and creative illustrations.

CPSIA information can be obtained at www.ICGtesting.com
Printed in the USA
BVOW07s1136161115

427316BV00016B/94/P